MW00795572

Halamar

HALAMAR

By

Gertrude Potter Daniels

CHICAGO NEW YORK
GEORGE M. HILL COMPANY

MDCCCC

HALAMAR

I

"There are chemical formations resulting from untoasted bread that are fatal to a weak stomach like mine," explained Madam Worthington to Dr. Maurice, "and there is a great difference in the way bread is toasted. That is one reason why I am kept so closely at home. My stomach denies me many pleasures and all freedom."

The lady made this statement expecting sympathy. She had made the statement so often that it had become second nature to listen for murmurs of concern to follow it. Her face had taken on the expression of resignation it always assumed at this point, but instead of murmurs her daughter-in-law remarked:—

"Toast keeps," a terse assertion, harmless in itself, but it brought a startled look to her husband's face.

"Until I began to eat toasted bread," went on the elder lady, with a defiant squaring of her shoulders and a superb ignoring of the remark, "my stomach rejected all food, and I was in a state bordering on physical collapse from sheer weakness. I owe much, very much, to toasted bread."

Maurice bowed profoundly. He had graduated from so many medical schools that he had begun to think independently. As a result he had lost faith in physic, and read character from complaints, and he seldom found the process misleading.

He sat opposite his hostess, and, while not in the habit of noticing what people ate, he now watched Madam Worthington unconsciously. He concluded that she could no longer be suffering from weakness. She had a remarkably good appetite.

Jean watched her, too, not at all because she was interested in Madam Worthington's diet; for she was not,—but after months of doing one thing it becomes a habit, and for a long time she had sat beside her and watched. She listened, too. She had such an intense dread of the crunching of that article which did not contain chemical formations, that she heard the sound distinctly. There seemed positively no escape from it. While she generally kept herself in hand, suffering in silence, sometimes she laughed outright, a jerky, grating laugh that a critical observer would have recognized at once as hysterical. But this always happened during some moment of suspended conversation. The result was a more telling silence and a withering glance from Madam Worthington. At this point Jean usually made matters worse by giggling and saying something inane that was seized upon by the guests as a way out of an uncomfortable situation.

"Young people nowadays have so little sympathy," continued Madam Worthington, helping herself plentifully to a dessert that was before her. At the same time she sent a half-glance toward the girl, a glance that was intended to show the littleness of the human mind. "Jean is a person of such excellent nerves that she lacks sensitiveness. She is self-centered as well, and, like the girls of the present generation, selfish and ungrateful."

Her son looked up impatiently. Jean flushed. Both knew what was coming, but in spite of having no "sensitiveness," Jean never became quite used to these frequent dissertations on her shortcomings. They were so unflinchingly personal.

"Girls in my day, Doctor, were brought up to be domestic and revere their elders. They were competent housekeepers before they became wives and helpmeets afterward. Now their one desire apparently is to emulate men. They attempt to carry out their masculine ideas by smoking, and wearing shirts. Their manners are vulgar, they know nothing of the feminine arts, and they are unladylike and unrefined."

Dr. Maurice was looking at his plate, and his hostess, looking also at hers, did not see the expression that had come into his eyes. He was a man who found good in the world and in people, so he protested :—

"I think, Madam, if you will allow me to say it, that you are a little severe." He was extremely courteous and seemed to be interested, but these two facts did not help him. Madam Worthington was unused to contradictions. In this case, too, she wanted to have it distinctly understood that she did not approve of her daughter-in-law, and she was willing to give her reasons. She was too proud to explain that her disapproval was based on the fact that the advice which she had volunteered had not been followed by her son in the matter of his marriage. But even the least suspicious of listeners soon discovered that this was the root of her antagonism. Now she lifted her head to a chilling height and said with much manner:—

"I am not at all severe. I am merely just,—just to myself and to my views, as well as to my rearing. Look at Jean! What does she do? And she is a fair example of the modern wife. Can she cook, or sew, or direct a house? Does she shoulder any responsibility? If she had married a poor man, would she have been in any sense a helpmeet?"

Jean took a hasty swallow of water, then she raised her eyes and looked her mother-in-law squarely in the face; too squarely; it foreboded desperation.

"Madam Worthington, it is unfair to show only my ignorance. It is quite true I do not know how to do any of these things you have mentioned. But how should I know? I never had a home, or a chance for experience in these things until I came here to you. I was anxious to learn. I was also more than willing to take my share of the responsibilities. I told you this, and apologized at the same time, you remember, for knowing so little about this sort of thing. You never were willing to give me any credit for what I had done and could do. The fact that I could support my mother, and sister, and myself, and that I had been the breadwinner for my family since I was a child, could not atone with you for my helplessness in directing a corps of servants. I have no wish to argue this subject, but I believe of the two, my work was greater and more necessary than yours. I supported, you spend."

The expression on the Doctor's face was very noticeable now, and it annoyed Madam Worthington.

"It is quite unnecessary to force your stage life into my home," she snapped. She would have said more but her physician had cautioned against getting overheated after a hearty meal.

"It is my defense," said Jean quietly, "otherwise I would have no wish to force it into your home." She was going to add, "or myself either," but she was afraid that it would hurt

Herbert; besides, it would have been impertinent.

At this point Herbert Worthington rose hastily. He looked nowhere in particular and his words came nervously. "May we have coffee served on the veranda, mother?" he asked.

Madam gave an unwilling consent. She had not finished much that she wished Dr. Maurice to hear. Perhaps his expression would have given place to another if she had been able to enlighten him with her entire version of this matter with Jean.

The four moved slowly out on to the veranda, where Jean stood a little distance from the others. The salt air came up cool and sweet from the ocean. Jean looked out across the great, tumbling mass of blue and white, and forgot her resentment. The world was beautiful, if the people in it were not. She stood there so long breathing in the delicious air that a bird on the highest branch of a tree near by turned its head, looked at her a moment, and then went on pluming itself, and singing an occasional snatch of song. But she was not watching the bird. She was hearing her husband move a chair. She knew how he was arranging pillows and foot-rests, and the wish passed through her mind that Herbert might sometimes show her the little attentions which he gave so freely to his mother. While she hated herself for the feeling, she was continually having the sensation of being left out — an interloper. She understood that it was her mother-in-law's wish to have her feel this; Herbert did not want it so. But now before she could brood she heard the sound of a horse cantering, and turned. The move brought her face into the clear sunlight.

"Oh, Dick, hello! I'm so glad you've come," she cried out to the man on the horse.

He took off his hat and waved it; then he pulled the animal up sharply and leaned over to pat its head.

"We are just having coffee out here. Come and join us."

'Do you want me?" He was bending over so far that his face was on a level with hers.

She laughed lightly. "You know," she said in a low voice.

When he had dismounted, they both stood watching the horse as the groom led it away.

By this time Madam Worthington had been established comfortably, even to a pair of binoculars close at hand with which to watch events that might happen out of the range of her spectacles. So Dr. Maurice and Herbert joined the other two. There was a little constraint in Worthington's manner as he shook hands with Dick Carrington, but Maurice clapped him on the shoulder, and his way of doing it was a caress. Dick was a great favorite with him.

"I have run away from my work. I should have gone to New York last week. I simply have no business being idle one moment," Carrington said, going toward Madam Worthington. "Your home is such an attractive one," he added, bowing over the hand that she held out.

The old lady looked up at him sharply. "Are you sure it is the home that is attractive?" she asked.

Carrington never blushed. His face was so bronzed that extra color would not have shown anyway. But he did not take life very seriously, and now he laughed unaffectedly.

"The home and all that lies therein. Literally the boards and lath and plaster can not be called alluring, I suppose. Even the pictures, and bric-à-brac, and works of art and all the rest that goes towards making up a charming whole would lose much of their charm without the life that people infuse into them. Of course I enjoy beautiful things in themselves and for themselves, but I spoke more from the idealic point of view." This was a long speech from Carrington. Thinking of it afterward he wondered just why he had spoken at such length. It sounded, too, like an explanation, yet he assured himself that he really had nothing to explain.

"It all follows out the law of suggestion," mused Maurice, who was a great believer in that law. "Have you never associated a thing with a person until the inanimate teemed with the thought and the feeling of its owner?" He had addressed no one in particular. He had an abstracted way of speaking, yet people always listened to him. "It is through that law of suggestion that we put ourselves in touch with the Creator. Ah, that is a wonderful power." He rolled out the word "wonderful" until it became replete with an intense meaning.

But because this mention of the Creator was not entirely conventional it was seized upon by Madam Worthington as a possibility for argument. She considered herself appealed to and regarded herself for the moment as

God's defender. "I do not agree with you," she put in testily. "The tendency of the age lies too much that way. All these idealistic views — what are they but an attempt to fill out laws for the expounding of sentimentality? Old fashioned ideas were not sentimental, and they still stand as solid foundations for good common sense. I am an advocate of the old school."

To her great disappointment the cudgel was not assumed by Dr. Maurice, for he never argued. He leaned back in his chair, not even flushing, and looked out at the sea. The immensity of it was reassuring.

"I am going down to the beach," announced Jean. She had been wandering up and down restlessly. Sometimes quiescence is an impossibility.

"May I go?" asked Carrington, a little hastily, then immediately feeling that he should not have asked so abruptly.

"Certainly. And you, Dr. Maurice, will you go?"

But Maurice had to start for town in a few moments and Herbert would not leave him, so Jean and Carrington went away together.

"I 'm glad they could n't," said Dick, vaguely.

She was silent, picking her way carefully down the steep bluff until they were half way to the beach. Then she stopped. "Dick, it has about come to the jumping off place," she began, abruptly. She was not referring to the bluff, but Carrington understood.

"I knew it would. You ought never to have left the stage. You had too much ability."

"It is n't that at all," she broke in, impetuously. "I understood what I was giving up when I did it. The stage means hard work, and struggles, and jealousies. I loved it, of course. It was my profession. But it is n't that. I am not regretting. It is her unfairness and — the toast."

A queer gleam came into Carrington's eyes. He wanted to say some things that he knew were not right. "Herbert ought to take you away," he exclaimed finally, with more force than the words warranted. Then he began to punch holes in the sand with the handle of his riding whip. "She is the most impossible person I know."

"That's it. He ought to give me a home that is mine," she went on, taking up the first part of his speech. "A place where I could study housekeeping in private and laugh away the mistakes with him. I suppose it is not in the least honorable, my talking to you about Herbert and his mother, but the mother does not spare me. 'An eye for an eye,' yet I never believed wholly in that either. But sometimes one has to talk, absolutely must. I keep still so long that I have to get relief occasionally, and let out my grievances. You see I can not understand her ways at all. She lives for, and is governed by, that house. She has no thought beyond it, no interest above it. I try to get used to its being in a constant state of upheaval. I try to think that a house is meant for that; that we build and furnish, not for comfort and peace, but for the privilege of continually cleaning and worrying. Once I remarked that this feature appeared unnatural. It was a mistake. For a moment I was stared at in deadly silence, then I was asked to be seated. Madam Worthington seated herself opposite to me. With great dignity and reserve she informed me that she was carrying out a system of generations of ancestors; this housekeeping was a trust, the carrying out of which had become a sacred duty; that at her death this task would fall upon her son's wife, and it was befitting that this wife should be prepared for the holy work. She explained this to me at great length, and all the while she was talking I had such an uncontrollable desire to laugh that I could n't entirely hide my amusement. It really was funny because she was so serious. Of course she saw that I was not impressed, and she was offended and asked with punctiliousness what my ideas were about housekeeping. It was a retaliation. I gave my ideas; at least the only ideas I had. I set forth the art of dusting and sweeping as it existed for stage business. I even went through a scene for her. Dick, that was the climax — a fatal climax. It did not reassure her at all. Stage housekeeping and New England housekeeping are not one and the same."

"Not at all," Carrington filled in the pause.

"She began from that moment to judge me altogether from the standpoint of an unworthy addition to tradition. I did not mind that, for in the main, it was ridiculous. I could have stood it easily. I could even have stood the toast, but because I was not crushed, she seemed exasperated and became insulting. She says things that are untrue and Herbert lets her talk. That hurts. She insinuates to everyone who comes here that I married him for money, and sometimes I think Herbert believes her. He has heard it so much. He is getting unreasonable and is so unlike himself."

"Damned cad," muttered Dick.

"No, he isn't. He is New England. Naturally he is not used to the kind of girl I represent. I think he hardly knows what to make of me. He has lived so long with his mother. I can't be circumspect or even dignified except for a few moments when a part requires it. Neither can I be elegant to strangers and slipshod to my own. I suppose I have been bumped into by people so hard all my life that it makes me free and easy. One gets away from elegance of manner after years of 'bumping.' His mother calls me vulgarly familiar; he calls it flirting. She sneers and he's jealous. I have tried to change, but it's no use. My manners are part of me, like my nose or my hair. I am not vulgar and I don't flirt—now."

"Well?" queried Dick.

"There we are. There is where I always land. 'Well.' You know that I am very fond of Herbert, really very fond, but these constant quarrels make me lose patience and courage. It has not been my way to live in quarrels. There come days when I think I would not mind leaving it all if it were not for Lucie. But it is a big question to decide; beside I believe in the stability of marriage vows."

She put this out as a kind of argument.

"When is Lucie coming home?" he asked, ignoring the remark.

"Very soon; and I had planned such a winter for her. A coming out party and society and all that. She is pretty, and she will have beautiful clothes. I am sure she will be a great success. She has the society temperament. You know it takes a combination of peculiar characteristics to make a successful society woman." There was an expression of amusement on Jean's face.

Carrington was watching her. "Hal, you have sacrificed enough for that girl," he said presently.

She looked up at him quickly. The care had all gone from her eyes. Neither one of them had heard the other man coming down the path that rose steep above them; nor did they know when he stopped only a few feet away. He was in plain sight if they had turned their heads. But they did not turn, and he, knowing that they had not heard, kept very still that his presence should not be known.

"Dick, you have not called me that since—" she stopped a moment, thinking.

"Since the night that you told me you were going to marry Worthington," he finished.

"Yes. It is a long time. You did not like it."

"Why should I have liked it?"

Jean made no immediate response to this. She had grown pale and looked tired.

"You know that I thought it was a shame to ruin your whole future the way you did. There is no getting around the fact that you had a glorious chance. I told you then as I tell you now, you considered Lucie too much — yourself too little. I believe in sisterly forethought; I do not believe in self-sacrifice." Carrington hesitated a moment, then went on slowly. "Besides, I cared a great deal for you, Hal, and, I suppose I have no right to say it, it was hard to give you up to him. . You see I was jealous, and a man is selfish when he is jealous. He can't see beyond his own sorrow and disappointment. It didn't make it a bit easier to know that you were getting a better fellow and one worthier of you than I could ever have been. I simply did not want him to have you. I thought then that I could not endure it."

Up to this time Jean had sat rigid and speechless under the torrent of the man's words. She had never known Carrington to show such feeling before.

Usually this was not his method of taking life. For some time she could not bring herself to a realization of what he was saying. But finally the tension went out of her whole body. Then she turned to him.

"Don't, Dick. Stop! This is not right," she said, hurriedly.

And just then the other man stepped down. "Carrington, I want Jean for a little while," he said.

II

Carrington rose immediately, scarcely glancing at Worthington, who stood stiffly erect and staring straight ahead.

The coming of the other man had been so abrupt and so unexpected that, for a moment, his presence brought a kind of terror into the girl's mind. After all, it is oftener the appearance of guilt rather than any actual wrongdoing, that influences a judgment.

Jean watched Carrington climb the bluff and disappear. She knew that with his going a silence must be broken, and in the talk to follow, a decision must be reached. This decision had been approaching for a long time. Now that it had come she shrank from the ordeal. It is not easy to reason over a serious problem with a man who is so jealous as to be blind to logic. Jean also realized that if he had overheard Dick's speech, nothing would ever convince her husband that there was no justification for his suspicions.

All at once the beauty of the day faded. The loveliness of the sea and the sky and the sweetness of the air grew oppressive as the gloom of her own unhappiness. She raised her eyes frankly to his, and the look in them should have set his mind at rest. She had nothing to withhold, nothing to evade.

He broke into his subject at once. At first his thought had been not to mention the overhearing of their conversation, but a moment's reflection altered his mind. So he began very gently, as if he had made a resolve to be kind to her.

"Jean, I do not want you to think I have been spying on you. Neither do I want you to be ignorant of the fact that I heard what Carrington has just said. I did hear, word for word; and, well, it was not altogether a surprise to me. I have known always that he cared for you, but I believed him too honorable to talk so openly of it. However, it makes no radical difference. It only brings matters to a crisis sooner than I expected. It has been coming on a long time — this crisis. I mean that some things have got to be settled between you and me. Of course you have felt this. I have known that you felt it."

An indescribable change had come over the girl's face, but he could not see that. He had pulled his hat down over his eyes so that he could see nothing very clearly. He waited barely a moment, perhaps expecting her to speak, but she was silent, and he went on again: —

"Long ago when I told my mother that you were the woman I wanted to marry, she said to me that you would not make me a good wife. She tried to explain that we had been brought up in such different atmospheres that we could never make a go of it. You would see and express one phase of life, I another. And they were such different phases. I did not argue the point with her; merely replied that I intended to marry you. Then my mother bowed her head. After all, I was a man and the head of my house, and she had no real right to interfere. But I had none of my mother's fears. I want you to understand and believe that. The only thing that did stand between me and absolute contentment was Dick Carrington. I saw even then what you did not, that Dick loved you. I also realized that you were very fond of him, and I saw danger in the attitude of mind that you exhibited. Of course you meant nothing by your easy manner of good fellowship. Still he was a bond between the old life you loved and the new life that you felt strange in. You had much in common with him — much more, in fact, than you had with me, and I felt this and dreaded it. I thought the matter over; it really was never out of my mind. I saw a way out of it, but I did not like to suggest it. You had promised to give up the stage entirely, and Carrington belonged to that part, and should have gone with it. I waited for you to suggest giving him up. It seemed such a small thing for me to ask. I had nothing against the fellow. He was gentlemanly and thoroughly agreeable, and I liked him; but frankly I was jealous of him. I have always been jealous of him, and as he says, 'jealousy makes a man very selfish.' Yet he seemed to have every charm that I lacked, except money."

Jean drew back with a sudden sharp movement. This time he gave her no chance to speak, but went on talking quickly. Perhaps he was afraid that if he hesitated he would lose the courage to say what was in his mind.

"During the year and a half that we have been married I have been thinking; oh, I have done a great deal of thinking, and I have found out many things. First, my mother was right; we do express the very extremes of life.

We are absolutely different. You were meant to do great things; the prosaicness I brought you into does not fit you. You were loyal enough to try, but it is of no use. I can see that now; no use at all. You do not belong here, and it has brought you closer to Carrington, for he represents what you love and regret. He was the one for you, not I. I never was the one. He could and would have kept you where you fitted and were contented."

"Herbert," she cried, and her voice had a strange thrill in it. She sat up very straight, her face growing white as she fully realized what he was saying.

But out of all he had said to her she could gather but one thought: He was ashamed of her. It was unbearable. She did not notice how closely he had followed her own words and ideas; they sounded so differently, coming from another. Worthington had taken no notice of her cry, although he was watching her. Presently he went on, still hurriedly:—

"I have always despised men who would not look things squarely in the face. I want to prove to both of us that I understand, and—look—I do not want you to put a wrong construction on what I say. I am trying to be honest, for I have no sympathy with evasions. Besides, in the end, honesty always wins. I know now that my money must have been an inducement because of your sister. I am not saying this because I blame you. While I have never been in need of money, that does not prevent my understanding how people can need it. Of course I do not believe that out of a purely personal selfishness you would have married me for financial reasons. If you had had only yourself to consider, you probably never would have married me at all. But the mistake has been carried far enough. I am going to free you. Like Carrington, I do not believe in self-sacrifice. I shall give you the protection of my name as long as you need that protection, and I shall settle a good income on you. But you will be free until the time comes when you wish to give up your freedom — to some one else."

There was pain in his voice and suffering in his face, but she felt nothing, understood nothing, except that she was being cast off; disposed of without hesitation or a qualm, as though she were some article of merchandise; and all because he believed her mercenary! And in love with Carrington! It was really this last that stung her.

She was too proud to defend herself even if she could have spoken, but her voice had left her, and her thoughts were too chaotic to talk logically or rationally. To be sure, she could have told him that she loved him, but it was no time to speak of love. At least this was her feeling. Perhaps if she had wholly understood his mood, she would have known that it was the precise moment to speak. But it seemed like flaunting in his face what he would not believe. He might even think it was a last hope resorted to because she was afraid to face the future without his money and the luxury it brought.

So she kept still, and his blood froze and everything grew black about him. In his agony to have her deny all that he had said, he misunderstood her silence, as men always misunderstand when they suffer. Until he was waiting for her to speak, he had been unconscious of how much he had said only to have her contradict and disprove.

"Jean, I shall miss you so." He put his hands across his eyes. His voice sounded like a cry.

"Don't," she said lightly, and her voice was higher than usual. "It is absurd to miss a person; especially the person that you send away from you as unfit to occupy the position you have put her in. There are many women more fit. You see I have thought on this subject too. There are women who cook, and dust, and sweep, and like upheavals and dry toast—perhaps even eat it. I mean the toast. Let your mother choose your next wife. Never go into a second matrimonial venture without her help. You can not but have confidence in her after this wonderful proof of her foresight, or rather her foreknowledge. You must marry a woman who can keep the ghosts of your ancestors quiet in the celestial sphere. I should rouse them to despair. Fancy your mother trying to enjoy Heaven while I was keeping her house. I am going up to her house now to pack. I do not need a week's notice like a serving maid," and she started up. The move was an abrupt one as though she followed out some sudden determination of her mind.

As she hurried away the sun went under a cloud. The brightness, too, had left her face. Or it may have been that the shadow of that cloud reflected itself there. Worthington made no effort to detain her. He was hardly conscious of what had happened. He knew that once, half way up the bluff, she stumbled as though she did not see well, but even then, he had no realization of matters. She went on and up swiftly, and finally disappeared.

As he sat thinking it over, he could not grasp it all. He knew she had said nothing and that he had said much, yet not what he had intended to say. At least he had not put the thing right. He had meant to be thoroughly unselfish and very kind, but instead of that he had given her the impression of wanting to be rid of her. This much was clear. Still, even though his words sounded that way, she should have divined how wretched he was. Surely by this time, having been his wife so long, she ought to know that he loved her.

The thought that he had made her suffer was becoming unendurable, for his heart was very tender toward her. If anyone had tried to explain that his neglect of Jean had caused her a moment's pain, he would have received the information with chilly incredulity.

After a little, Worthington's thoughts went to Ruskin. He had an immense admiration for that man. The nobility of Ruskin's sacrifice had appealed to him years before, and although he would not have acknowledged it even to himself, he had patterned largely after that sacrifice in this episode with Jean. Only it had turned out more seriously than he had expected.

Worthington had frequently asserted that unfitness in unmarried life and continued suffering from that unfitness was as vulgar as it was unnecessary. He had been brought up to shun vulgarity as commonplace and low, and no matter what else the Worthingtons might have been, there was nothing in their pedigree that belonged to the unclassed. So in a way he was carrying out a theory, perhaps a hobby, but now that it had been tried, he was constantly being brought back to that first conclusion. Somehow he had not arranged things as romantically as Ruskin had.

For a long time the man sat there on the sand; his thoughts miserable and morbid; his heart heavy and over-burdened.

The first shadows of evening were coming across the land when he finally arose. He was stiff and sore, but he worked his way up the bank as Jean had hours before. He decided that they must have another talk. He would ask Jean if she really preferred Carrington or freedom. This made him feel easier, for he knew well enough what she would say. In the depths of his heart Herbert Worthington was very sure of his wife, but jealousy is a thick crust to break through.

His mother was standing on the porch waiting for him. She shielded her eyes with one hand; in the other she held the binoculars.

"Herbert," she called, "you are very late. It is not wise to sit on the sand so long. I have been uneasy."

"I was with Jean," he replied, forgetting how long it was since she had left him.

His mother looked at him curiously. "Jean came up hours ago. She left on the five o'clock train. Do you know where she has gone?"

III.

By the time Jean reached Boston, the wind had veered abruptly from the west to the east, and was blowing in sharply from the sea. It stung her face and she gave an involuntary shiver as she stepped out of the station to call a cab. By hurrying she could catch the night express to New York. She explained this to the driver, had her trunk put on the box beside him, and promised him an extra fare if he succeeded in getting her to the other station in time.

There were no definite plans in her mind; only an intense desire to get away from Boston. It was a city that she had never wholly liked; now it had become a place of dread from the very strength of its associations. She realized that she could never experience any further peace of mind in this home of her married life, yet, as she thought of it, there came more of resentment than sorrow at the circumstances which were forcing her away. It was the unfairness of the thing. She had been very devoted to Herbert. Her devotion had carried her to such lengths that she had never been quite happy unless he were with her. He knew this, too. Now she was leaving him; putting him away out of her life. No one could tell what the end might be.

She went over this again and again all through that drive, and loneliness increased upon her until she was overwhelmed with the burden of it.

When Jean was finally settled on the train it began to rain. The gloom outside expressed the gloom of her own thoughts, and in a way, was comforting. The weather at times is an excellent sympathizer. She sat close by the window, and people watching her would have thought her intent upon the dreary landscape that spread itself like a map from the car window into the distance;

but she was doing nothing of the sort. She was staring anywhere, everywhere, but seeing nothing. As it grew dark, so dark that the country was a blur, and the glass reflected her own image, she was still staring.

There is something uncanny about getting into a large city in the early morning. The vague mutterings and stretchings and noisy yawns of an awakening creature are awesome. Jean left the train as the sun was sending its first rays through the mist that came in from the sea and drifted across the city. She groped her way out of the smoky station into the vapory uncertainty of the streets, and found herself missing Herbert again. Even here in her old camping ground his absence seemed unnatural. Married life had taken all feeling of independence from her. She experienced a sense of gratitude that, added to all the rest of her unhappiness, there was not the hopelessness of coming alone into a strange land. For, after all, New York was her home. She was also thankful that she had money enough for present needs.

She bargained with the man who drove her to the hotel, and she had a distinct understanding with the clerk as to the price of her room. It had been so long since she had been obliged to practice the small economies of life that it seemed odd.

"I expect," she thought to herself, as she unpacked her things, "that I shall be reduced to a room the size of a small closet, and a chafing dish, before I get through with it. There is no denying that money is a great factor in life."

She began spreading her things around one by one. It is remarkable how a few silver toilet articles, some pictures and a book or two can change the appearance of a room. She stood for a few seconds critically contemplating the rejuvenation, but evidently her mind was elsewhere, for presently she sat down, saying disconsolately: "I must find something to do. I certainly will not take one cent that belongs to him."

This thought of his money moved her strongly. It had become dreadful to her, for it would always stand with her as a representation of ill feeling and sorrow and separation. Her heart beat heavily, and she caught her breath in a sob. She had realized so little just what had happened; perhaps because she had not stopped to think. It had come so suddenly. But now as she stood there, a sensation of agony came over her. She pressed her hands together so tightly that the fingers interlocked and hurt. "It is the foreverness," she cried out sharply. It was in this way that the understanding came to her of what this separation meant. For a long time she sat still in her chair, absorbed in the dreary conception of what the future held for her.

"I will write to Dick," she thought; then her face flushed with a guilty remembrance of what Herbert had said. But it had changed the current of her revery and eased the tension of her overstrained nerves. She was very pale and very tired when she finally rang the bell and ordered her coffee served in her room. Her energy had deserted her, and she had no wish to meet the new faces that would stare at her in the breakfast room.

Jean Worthington was not a person of hesitations, but rather eminently active, and the more she thought over the situation, the more certain she became that on Lucie's account, an apartment would be necessary. She had seen enough of hotels to know that they were not desirable as an abode for a young and pretty girl. So she hunted up the place where she had lived before. It was on Forty-second street, and not at all a quiet neighborhood, but it had been convenient to the theatre. Now it seemed to her like an old friend. The very shops around it were homelike; even some of the faces were familiar, and it was all so little changed and so homelike that she grew more cheerful and light-hearted, and greeted the old janitor with an enthusiasm that thawed his dignity.

The building itself was of a forbidding aspect. It was stiff and straight, and the brick had changed color in spots, but when Jean found that the apartment above her old one was for rent, she did not hesitate a moment. It seemed like a gift of good omen. It was furnished, too, rather gaudily, and not at all in good taste; still it accomplished a great deal in saving expense.

"You 'll find changes here," the janitor announced. "The top floor is took by four young men, and one of 'em writes plays, sort of in your line of work. Perhaps you will like to know him. They 're going to stay some time, if their money holds out."

Jean expressed her pleasure at knowing they had hopes of staying so long, and thought perhaps she would like to meet the one who was in her line of work. Then she added, as an after thought, that as she was living quietly now, she did not expect to meet many people, or entertain extensively.

After she had told him of her decision to take the rooms, she talked about the arrangements for cleaning, and the payment of the rent. When there was positively nothing more to be said, she went for a walk. For a time she kept to the cross streets, because in spite of her determination to practice small economies, she did not find Fifth avenue congenial. The beautiful things she saw filled her with a sort of discouragement, for there were mental comparisons that would crop up.

"I must have very expensive tastes," she thought. "Cheap things are not at all attractive. I hate cheap things. Yes, I know that I am extravagant and selfish." And the walk became so much of a failure that she went back to the hotel, depressed and uncertain.

She was taking the pins out of her

hat, and at the same time looking at Herbert's photograph, when a bell-boy brought her a card. She held it up to read her husband's name, and her first thought was the oddity of having his presence announced to her in this way. Then she wondered why he had followed her.

"I will be down in a moment," she said, her eyes still on the card. After the boy had gone, she laid the bit of pasteboard down gently, and put the pins in her hat again.

A woman is always more self-possessed than a man. She found him pacing the floor rather wildly, his hands nervous and twitching. Jean, on the contrary, was very quiet. She greeted him with a calm smile that loosened the frenzied grip with which he had seized her hand and froze the hope that had been growing warm within him.

He looked years older. She noticed this at once, though naturally she said nothing. Nor did Jean's eyes flinch when they met his, and no one, least of all he, would have guessed at the longing that had come over her and the tumult that raged within her.

He had come to ask forgiveness; to beg her to go back. But as he looked at her he had a feeling that the coming was ill-timed. So the words and even the thought died unspoken.

"Jean, I have been so worried—so, unhappy," he began, brokenly. The words were so different from what she expected to hear that she answered at random.

"Why?" she asked. "I have been very proper. I do not forget that I bear your name. I expect to leave here next week and go to my apartment. You remember the old apartment, of course. We used to be happy there. The one I have now is on the floor above. It is all rather strange, isn't it?"

"Jean, we are both foolish—both wrong. It has been too insignificant a thing to cause a separation."

"I had no wish for a separation. You found I did n't fit, and you were quite right; I did n't. I saw it as plainly as you did. I had no thought of such a remedy as this; still I knew there must be a change."

The man caught at this as a gleam of hope.

"What change, Jean? What was the change you wished?" he begged.

"A home of my own. A place where I could be the mistress absolute and complete. Your mother dislikes and disapproves of me, and, Herbert, I am not fond of her. Why should I be? She has belittled me and insulted me from the moment I entered her house as your wife. She has had no consideration for me; showed no kindness toward me. Neither on my account, nor for Lucie, would I consent to live with her any longer."

"I think you misjudge her. Still, a home like this, Jean, I could not promise it, now. It would leave my mother so alone. She depends on me, you know that, and she is my mother. You make it very hard for me." He hesitated a moment, then he asked suddenly: "If I could make this arrangement that you ask, would you agree to one thing?"

"What?"

"That Carrington should never come into that home of yours?" He put the question feverishly and without looking at her. But she watched him intently — so intently that presently she forced his eyes to meet hers.

"No," she said.

A dull color suffused his face. "After all, this separation is best," he burst out angrily, forgetting his purpose in coming. "It is no mistake. It is not trivial, either. But be quite sure on one point, Jean, this thing can never be healed by concessions on my part alone. You have something to do — something to sacrifice as well as I. And the sacrifice of that man is the thing that I demand."

"It is not necessary to go all over

this again," said Jean wearily. "I have not demanded anything from you, neither have I asked any sacrifice or concession. I wish simply what I believe is right and fair. After all, I should come before your mother, you know. I am willing, and always have been, to do anything for you that is reasonable. When you demand something foolish I see no crime in refusing. Dick is a dear, good friend. I shall not give him up to satisfy an unjust suspicion. You have nothing else against him."

There came a pause. Herbert Worthington stood awkwardly before her. A belated remembrance of Ruskin came to him again.

"Have you money enough for the present? I will open an account for you to-day at the National bank," he said, tactlessly.

She looked up at him, and her eyes flashed fire. "I would rather starve than take one cent that belongs to the Worthingtons. I can never express to you how I loathe your money," she said.

And he left her with the breach widened instead of bridged, as he had intended, and as she had hoped.

IV

When Jean took possession of the apartment, the furnishings seemed more unendurable than ever. She had a distinct notion that they were loud enough to openly proclaim their inferiority, and while she assured herself that she was not at all ashamed of having to economize, she did not feel that this made it necessary to announce her poverty by surrounding herself with vulgar imitations of good things.

"Perhaps I was rather precipitate in taking this apartment. By the time I have packed away all the things I don't like, there won't be much left but the walls and the beds," she mused, scowling at some huge dishes of artificial fruit that stood in the dining room. Beside these were some platters, great, ungainly things with fish and game done in porcelain. The animals were life size, and were spread out on their sides in stony and uncomfortable attitudes.

She concluded to start the re-arranging with these, and after they were safely hidden in the depths of a large box which the janitor had brought her, she collected the bunches of paper flowers of marvelous hues, and the queer plaques and strange impossible pictures with hideous gilt frames and all the other things that were maddening in color and design. She spent an entire morning wrapping all these things with excelsior and placing them cautiously on the fish and game.

"It is a combination that could easily cause a spontaneous combustion," she remarked to the janitor who had come to nail on the cover. But he did not understand.

After they had been taken away, Jean sighed with actual relief, although there was still a great deal to be desired. The drawing room paper, for instance, with its black background and splotchy pink roses grinning all over it, was neither pleasant nor natural. "I wonder who could have had this place and what the man did for a living," she said aloud. Just then there came a preliminary knock at the door followed almost immediately by the entrance of the knocker. The man walked in blandly.

"Well, Hal, getting fixed?" he said, and from the way he spoke one would have thought that he belonged there. But she looked up at him, startled.

"Dick, how did you know I was here?" she asked.

"The janitor. What a devil of a wall!" he said, gazing at the paper.

"But the janitor—How did you happen here? He could n't have sent you word unless he knew you." She was not definite, but that did not interfere with his understanding.

"That 's just it. A mutual acquaintance. He knows me and I know him. I live up here—three other fellows who are not quite sane and I."

"The four young men, and one writes plays," repeated Jean, remembering the janitor's information.

"Omar writes plays," assented Carrington. "Hal, what are you going to do with this wall? You certainly are not endeavoring to live it down."

Carrington went up to it and felt of it gingerly. It was like him to ignore events. It was like old times, too, his wandering around in her rooms and suggesting things. For the first time since she had left her husband's home, Jean felt easy. But there was a hint of wistfulness in her eyes that Carrington saw and understood.

"Did you know the people who lived here? I was just wondering about them." She was falling into his mood.

"Certainly. He was a real estate man, and she, well, she was a woman with a dog. I should like to write about a woman and a dog. It would be the great American novel that is so talked of. They hated us—those two."

"Why?" asked Jean, pressing down on a fragile, three-legged chair to see if it was safe.

"Probably because we hated them. Hal, for Heaven's sake tell me what you are going to do with this wall?" He thumped a bunch of buds, then rubbed his fist.

"I shall leave it to you and the other three, Dick," she replied. Then she stood facing him. She felt that something ought to be said; not much, but something. "Be quite honest; have I been stubborn or foolish?" she began.

"No," he answered, fiercely. Before he came in he had made up his mind to be strictly neutral both in voice and action. But almost immediately this resolve was forgotten.

"But for Lucie's sake; should n't I have gone back for her sake? I don't want her to see the unhappy side of life, nor do I want her 'bumped,' and I can't give her much else here. It won't be as it would have been in Boston; I mean the people, and she expected that." Her voice was anxious, and she was very conscious that to anyone else this communication would have appeared vague and indefinite. For this reason it was a relief to talk to a man who understood without details. She felt incapable of giving details about this trouble.

"There 's honor among thieves," he answered, solemnly, "and while we are not exactly thieves, still we are honorable. Lucie may not meet the people who do society, but she will know the ones who do things, and of the two, Hal, I prefer the latter. They may not possess such intelligence of manner, but their intelligence of morals is larger. You will find that the child will be very safe, and, if she has sense, very happy and contented, too."

Jean gazed steadily at him for an instant, but the expression of solemnity did not leave his face. It restored her confidence and set her right in her mind. At once she left the subject and asked about the other three. Who they were and what.

Carrington turned his back to the wall, and deciding that his length and weight were too great for safety elsewhere, sat down on a hassock, facing the girl.

"We joined forces because we were too poor to live separately; but instead of four we are really three. Iky Marston and Jo Manvel don't go singly. They're collective. They write — collaborate. They can't think apart because they never have, and there is a good deal in habit. They are homely; so excessively homely that they keep together to buoy each other up. They have buoyed each other up in this way since they were boys. The result is that they think alike, act alike, have the same view point, and are good stuff. They are sensitive and shy. I call them 'my plants.' But they will make a future. One book has been successful — for the publisher.

"Then Omar — he is all they are

not and some that they are. He is the playwright. He has three good manuscripts, and is at work on a fourth, but he has no pull. No manager will accept those plays either singly or in a bunch."

"Why?" put in Jean. She had picked up some mending and was drawing her chair nearer the window.

"Grewsome and too hard to act. That's what they say, though I believe it is merely an excuse. But he is good stuff, too, only poor, devilish poor.

"That brings it up to me: painter at times, dauber and dreamer mostly, also poor — except during spells. My money comes like malaria, intermittently. In fact, we all get our money that way. That's how we get on, for we don't all receive at once. If you will give me something to throw, I will bring the other fellows down. I told them what I expected them to do if they heard a thump under their feet. They are probably listening for it now; I can't hurt the ceiling, you know."

He looked about him, but seeing nothing available, he took off one of his slippers and then stood up. Three times he threw it up against the ceiling. After the second whack there was the sound above them of moving feet, and by the time Carrington's slipper was back in its proper place and he had gotten out to the door, the three men stood there. Omar was in front, Iky and Jo, side by side, behind.

V

Carrington was not an advocate of formality, so he introduced the men by an announcement. "My friends," he remarked, accompanying the words with a sweeping gesture that included them all. He believed this was quite sufficient until he saw the puzzled look on Jean's face. Then he individualized by pronouncing with great solemnity the name of each and his profession. There was such a subtle air of good fellowship about everything Carrington did, that it put people at ease in spite of themselves.

Jean met the men in the same spirit in which she had been presented, and laughed so contagiously at the introduction that they all caught the infection and laughed with her. This placed them on a good basis and made Iky and Jo feel singularly personal.

They advanced separately to shake hands, and even forgot for the moment that here was a new person to become accustomed to their plainness.

"How did the thump sound?" asked Carrington, as they followed Jean into the parlor.

"Delicate," said Iky, and his voice was gentle and low. "Your boot?"

"No, slipper," replied Dick. Then with a wave of his arms he called attention to the wall. "It's been put in our hands — this. What shall we do with it?"

"I'll lend my plays. I think I have manuscript enough to cover it," suggested Omar.

"It would queer the house. Won't do," answered Dick. "We would have the janitor telling stories about headless bodies and drowned women."

"Plaster the manuscripts on loosely, then pull 'em off when the wall begins to creak. You'd find the paper pale with horror, and a pale background with pink buds would n't be bad." Jo spoke quickly and ended abruptly with his voice still on the upward inflection. It gave Jean a feeling of uncertainty.

"Paint it, Dicky," put in Iky.

"I could turn it into a thunder storm," assented Dick, "except that it would keep Jean in a state of worry for fear the furniture would get wet. It would n't be easy, either, living in a mackintosh. They smell disagreeably and take away one's appetite. Speaking of appetite, can't we have some tea, Hal? Where's your caddy? Iky, take the kettle out and fill it."

Carrington and Iky set about making the tea, and Omar and Jean went to toast bread. So Jo, to be useful, set a table and hunted around in impossible places for cups.

"May I read one of your plays some day?" asked Jean, looking up from the stove and smiling at Omar.

"Omar was cutting a loaf of bread. He gouged it now in his enthusiasm.

"Oh, will you?" he cried. "It is the one thing I would have asked.

You know so well, and I have never had anyone to judge for me." His face flushed and his eyes grew very eager.

"I am not a good judge, because I can never get away from my own feelings. If a thing appeals to me I like it, even when it may present very few good points to anyone else. You must not count on my judgment."

"But you know whether it will act or not. Oh, I should like to write a play for you!" he exclaimed.

A strange look crossed her face, but just then Carrington's voice came rolling in to them from the other room. "What's happening to the toast? The tea is strong enough to walk, and Jo is going stark mad over the cups. Hurry up!"

Omar stacked the bread that was still untoasted into a pyramid, and hurried in, balancing the plate cautiously. Jean followed, carrying a small pitcher of cream.

"I know who cut this," said Iky,

eyeing the plate as Omar sat down.

"What characters were you slaughtering?" asked Dick. "I have never spoken of it before because I am sensitive, but I feel like a cannibal when Omar has charge of the culinary department. He never manipulates food. It's always people. He works out all his tragedies that way. The thought is ghastly, and we all know that thoughts are things."

They all acquiesced promptly, although none of them was quite certain what Carrington was attempting to say. Presently he looked at the men who were standing around awkwardly, and advised them to take seats on the floor to save the chairs. At once Jean remarked that the furniture was insured This relieved Dick's mind, and they sat down stiffly on the miniature arrangements that served for chairs, and wondered who would break down first. They all took their tea clear. Jean looked up curiously. "What an idea!" she said.

"Saves money," announced Jo. At least Jean took it for an announcement, although Jo's voice rose upward and floated away, without falling. "We like it now."

After tea the men, apparently of one accord, arose and standing close together, broke into song — a serenade. Dick led and they sang in time, but the tone and tune varied.

"I believe in music," explained Carrington. "It elevates the soul and keeps the thoughts pure. We sing this the last thing every night. Sometimes it comes pretty late. We used to do it loudly and with force until a tenant objected. Now we are more gentle. If you listen though you will be apt to hear it, Hal."

Jean promised. Then she urged them to drop in often, as she was lonely and would depend on them to cheer her. They in their turn promised, said good night to her as they would have said it to each other, and climbed the stairs.

"They are dear, good fellows," said Jean, then sighed, for after all there was desolation in her heart, and she missed Herbert.

The next week, Lucie came. Jean went alone to the dock. Carrington wanted to be there to help with Lucie's trunks, but somehow Jean felt that it would be easier to explain things without him, and said so frankly.

She was anxious to see her sister; so anxious that she walked up and down nervously, straining her eyes for the first sight of the steamer. But in her anxiety there was uneasiness. A year of luxury was apt to make a great change in a girl's disposition — especially a young girl. It is a much simpler matter to go up than down, and although Jean had given her the upward start, this would be forgotten when she must come down again.

She felt this so intensely that there was a question in her mind as to how Lucie would accept the changed conditions. It was while her thoughts were centered on this that she noticed a murmur and a closing together of the crowd. She looked up with a start to see the boat swinging into sight.

It was all a confusion of many people at first. But presently she saw Lucie standing far up in front, the wind blowing her skirts tight about her, her handkerchief fluttering above her head. Then a great lump came into Jean's throat that did not go until after she held the girl close in her arms and sobbed hysterically once or twice. After that it was easier, and she let go her hold and looked at her sister critically.

She was changed certainly. There was an air of elegance about her that made her a little unapproachable, and the expression of her face was self-possessed, or haughty, according to the way one saw expressions. She carried herself with an extreme and aristocratic grace, and was evidently surprised at Jean's deep emotion.

She had a great many trunks and she knew a great many men. Also she spoke French incessantly, catching herself up every once in a while and plunging into English. It was as though she constantly forgot that she had left France.

Bit by bit Jean's uneasiness increased. A chill struck at her heart. She gave a little uncontrollable shiver, and Lucie turned to her at once. "Cherie, you are cold. Take this. It is very warm." And she laid a tiny French affair that she had been carrying in her hands about Jean's shoulders. It was strongly perfumed and very pretty, but wholly useless, and Jean had an unaccountable desire to throw it off. It was a feeling that she was ashamed of, so she fought it down.

By this time Lucie had caught the eye of an inspector, and was looking up into his face with an adorable smile. He examined her trunks, and she sat perfectly still during the proceeding, and let him look and handle and disarrange. Jean decided that this required great courage. By the few glimpses that she caught she knew those boxes were brimful of delicate, dainty, fragile, unpractical things. She finally said: —

"Lucie, I should be in a fever if those things were mine. That man will ruin them."

Lucie laughed; a sliding scale that sounded musical but did not mean anything. "There are many things there that belong to you. Come, he has finished. You are charming," she said to the inspector, then with a little courtesy, "Merci."

Jean had not come to the boat in a carriage, the expense was too great. So she led Lucie out to the street where there were a dozen vehicles in readiness, and left her sister near the door while she inspected the assortment. They were poor specimens to look at and worse to ride in, while the horses had an appearance of extreme dejection.

Lucie watched Jean talking to one of the drivers. He gesticulated a great deal and she talked a great deal. Lucie continued to watch, and although her eyes were lustreless, her face expressed a surprised interest that increased into lively concern when she found that she was expected to occupy so poor a conveyance. Somehow she felt that her dignity was being humiliated, and it was with an air of exaggerated submission that she took her place on the springless seat. She did not discuss the situation, however. In fact there came a decided pause that prolonged itself into a discomforting silence. Jean felt that this should not be so, and it led her to say: –

"Lucie, you got my letter?"

"Which one, Cherie? I have had many letters."

"The one about Herbert and me." It came out hard.

"Surely; why not?" asked Lucie, lightly.

"And you did not blame me?"

"No, certainly not. I prefer New York."

Jean gave a laugh. Carrington would have understood that laugh. It was very near a sob.

"I am so glad, dear. I was afraid you would be disappointed. It has troubled me a great deal."

Lucie made no response, and Jean leaned far back in the seat and was quiet. Perhaps after all she had misjudged her sister.

When they stopped at the apartment, she sat up with a cheery, "Here we are, Lucie."

At this the girl sat up too, and looked out. Surprise and dismay were suddenly reflected in her face. "Jean, this is where we used to live."

"Yes, dear."

"I expected that you had a house. Herbert is rich."

"Lucie, I thought you understood. Herbert and I have separated."

"Certainly, but he supplies you with money, does he not?"

"No," said Jean sharply, and there was something in her face that warned the other that she had said enough. They left the wretched carriage silently. A great fear was suddenly growing in Lucie's mind. Still not speaking, they went up into the apartment. There Lucie gave one look around her.

"Ask the maid to make me some tea," she said, pulling off her gloves. They were long, white new ones; verv white and very new.

"I have no maid, Lucie. I can not afford one." Jean was watching the way she crumpled up those gloves.

"Will you kindly explain to me how you live?" Lucie's voice was not pleasant.

It roused Jean. "We live as we used to live; as you always lived until my husband's money sent you abroad and ruined you. We do our own cleaning and make our own beds. We cook our breakfast and luncheon as best we can, and dine out. More than that, before long we will both have to work. Outside work, I mean, for the money that I have in bank will not keep us long, even in the frugal way in which we are to live,— and I suppose we must live," she finished, desperately.

Lucie got up. She walked across the room in a fashion intended to be hopeless, but to an outsider it would have looked very theatrical. Suddenly she turned, and there was intense anger in both her voice and manner.

"And this is what you have brought me back into, is it? Slavery, drudgery, humiliation; you who could give me money and carriages and nice things — things that I expected and needed. Yes, needed. I will not stand this; do you hear? I will not cook! I will not work? There is neither need nor necessity for it, and I am not used to it. I am delicate and pretty, and if you were not selfish and stubborn and brutal you would not so much as suggest this thing to me. I will go to Herbert myself — or you must. I won't live like this. Do you know how I feel towards you? I hate you! Yes, I hate you, and I am glad I have said it." Her voice had become shrill, and her face worked with fury until there were no signs of beauty in any one of her features.

But her acting and temper counted for nothing. She saw this after one glance into her sister's set, white face. Her fury became a frenzy at the very helplessness of the whole thing, and with a quick letting go of her body, she fell upon the floor, face downward, and lay there sobbing and beating with her hands.

VI

An hour later Carrington came. When he looked into Jean's haggard face he turned away. He saw that Lucie's return had resulted about as he expected, and Jean's evident suffering filled him with resentment against her sister.

Jean held up her hand. "Hush, she is lying down — asleep, I hope. Poor child," she said, and led him into the parlor.

The four men and Jean had covered the walls with a dainty creton that hid the paper and softened the other things in the room. They had worked hard to accomplish an appearance of attractiveness.

"It was a mistake, Dick, a wretched mistake. She thought the separation meant simply living apart and keeping up two establishments — one for Herbert, one for me. She did n't realize that I had any pride, and she can't see why I refuse his money. She thinks it is all selfishness on my part. I suppose it is, in a way. Still, I will not take his money."

Just then Lucie's voice came out plaintively. "Are you alone, Jean?"

"No, dear, Dick is with me. Will you come and see him?" Her voice was very tender.

Lucie thought she would. Perhaps seeing some one would change the current of her thoughts. She was so accustomed to company in Paris, and her home coming had been so unusual. It would take her some little time to get used to this different mode of life. They would understand that this was so very different. So the other two sat and waited. They did not talk because they could not. There was but one subject on their minds.

Presently Lucie appeared. She had put on an exquisite tea gown of pale pink with quantities of lace. Her face was white, but quite undisturbed. She walked languidly as though she were not strong.

"It is a pleasure to see you again," she said, but her eyes did not exhibit pleasure, nor did her manner. She was very self-possessed.

Carrington bowed profoundly. It saved his speaking at once; it also hid the contempt that crept into his eyes.

"Is n't Jean odd?" went on Lucie, quite willing to argue private matters, and all the time she spoke, she gave the impression of being unused to English words. "She has ideas about money. Such peculiar ideas. I think it is a pose. Jean is so full of the dramatic that she acts in spite of herself. But I don't act, and I don't care to be one of her company. I am not fit to work, and she ought to understand this. I must have money and amusement. I am so inclined to grow morbid if I have no amusements."

"We have amusements. We sing serenades. Perhaps you would like to hear us," suggested Carrington, trying to be natural.

"Ah, how charming! Who sings?"

"We four — really three. Iky and Jo, Omar, and yours truly."

"Omar? What a strange name." A bit of interest crept into her monotonous voice.

"Yes, we always call him Omar because none of us could learn to pronounce his last name. At times when another name is necessary I introduce him as Smith. Do you want to see him? Usually a thump brings them all, but the plants are out for an airing, so only he will answer." Dick had pursued the subject because her interest in it was the first thing he could seize upon as tangible.

Lucie looked condescending. "You are so odd," she said, then laughed her sliding scale again.

Omar came, but not alone. Dr. Maurice was with him, and he looked worried. He ignored Dick's question of when he had arrived, because he did not hear it, which was unlike Maurice.

"Let them go in there," he said, keeping hold of Jean's hand and speaking to Carrington. "I want to say something if you will allow me."

Omar had joined Lucie and sat facing her. She looked very beautiful and very fragile. Jean wondered how she could recover so quickly and so completely from the effects of her outburst. Her eyes were clear and her face showed no trace of tears, temper or disappointment.

Maurice still held her hand. "My dear, you are not well," he said in his great, gentle voice. "Yet I must add to your burden, for speaking at once may be kindness in the end. It is rumored that there is trouble at the Continental bank."

Jean gave a start, and the little light in her face went out, leaving it very white.

Maurice watched her. "I feared your money was there. Dick, we will go and see if it is too late."

"Shall I take Omar?" asked Carrington.

"No, let him stay. Lucie will forget all her unhappiness if she has him." There was no bitterness in her voice, only sorrow. Lucie's character had not been difficult to fathom.

So Maurice and Carrington went away and Jean counted the minutes after they had gone. She could hear Lucie's even tones and peculiar pronunciation. She knew, too, how Omar was sitting there motionless, and admiring the perfection of her beauty and the harmony of her gown.

All the while Jean was walking up and down wondering what the loss of her money would bring, and full of foreboding as to the effect upon Lucie.

The evening came on dreary and cold. Jean lighted the lamps and continued her walk. Omar was still contented. He was telling Lucie of his hopes and ambitions. The idea made Jean smile. Other people's hopes and ambitions in connection with Lucie was an incongruity.

It was nearly seven o'clock when the men came back. She did not ask a word. Carrington went directly to her and put both arms about her.

"Dear old Hal," he said with a pathetic break in his voice.

"All gone?" she asked, faintly.

"Nothing to be had just now; for many months even. Perhaps later; there may be a payment later. The bank is closed. We stood in line for hours. Poor devils!"

"The work has come sooner than I expected," was all she said, but Carrington felt her grow cold, and he could not meet her eyes.

After a little he took Omar and Maurice away. And when they were gone, Jean told Lucie all that had happened and all that it meant. The way that she told it held Lucie from another outburst. But the girl cried a great deal, and finally fell asleep in Jean's arms, still sobbing.

VII

For the next few weeks Jean did little else but seek work. It was rather a useless and profitless business. There was only one profession that she knew, and that she would not take up while she held the name of Worthington. It had been her promise to Herbert. Lucie begged and pleaded until Jean in desperation shut her off, saying peremptorily, that she would not ask Herbert for money, neither would she act without his permission; and that she was tired of hearing about the matter.

Still the subject of money was becoming awkward. It was Carrington who came to the rescue. He took Lucie for a model and paid her twenty-five dollars a week.

Another artist asked to paint a portrait of Jean. He wanted her to pose in one of the characters that she had created before her marriage. Perhaps he was far-sighted enough to see that the time must come when as Jean Halamar she would return to the stage and fame. Then, if not before, the picture might bring him notice. To himself he said "renown." At any rate it was a speculation that looked safe.

So she posed, and was paid for the sittings, but she could not get over the idea that, after all, it was a charity arrangement.

One day she received a letter from Madam Worthington. It was an insulting letter. Reading it took her back into that other world, and except for Herbert, she was thankful, very thankful, that she was out of it.

The letter was entirely about Herbert; his unhappiness and brooding over Jean; how, if she had any delicate sensibilities, she ought to see that an absolute divorce was the thing. This separation meant nothing. It was simply a barrier to Herbert's future.

"I feel sure," Madam wrote, "that after leaving your husband's home and going to live under the protection of another man, you will see that a return to the Worthingtons is quite impossible. Herbert feels this."

Then she insinuated that his affections were placed in another direction, and that freedom would be most acceptable.

Jean felt a tightening about her heart as she read.

"Men are inconstant, of course, but I did not believe he would be consoled so quickly," she thought.

"She did not answer the letter just then. She could not. Instead she put it in a drawer as something to think over and decide upon carefully.

She was sitting idly when Omar called outside of the door and asked if she would see him. She welcomed him with absolute relief. He had a manuscript, and he looked hopefully at her idleness.

"May I read? I have just finished

it. I want your opinion, your sincere opinion."

She smiled up at him.

"It won't bore you?" he asked.

"No, you don't know how glad I am to listen."

"And you have time?"

"All the time in the world," she said, settling back on the chair.

Omar had the knack of reading well. Probably because he felt what he wrote. At first Jean studied him. His gauntness and the hollows under his eyes touched her. He looked tired; yes, and hungry, too. And at times his body twitched as though the nerves were snapping under too great a tension. But presently she forgot him in the play. It was immensely strong. Sometimes repelling, but it held her attention. The climax was fearful and grewsome, as Carrington had told her, but it was powerfully worked out.

The instincts of the dramatic rose in her. She sat up straight, stiff, her face working itself into the very feeling of what he read. She saw it, lived it, acted it, and when he had finished, she sank back, limp and unnerved.

For a long time neither one spoke. The strain had affected them both. Still without speaking, she went to her desk and wrote. It was a letter of introduction to Richmond, her old manager, and in it she recommended his play. She signed the note, "Jean Halamar Worthington." It was the first time she had used her stage name since the "Worthington" had been added.

"That is my answer — my opinion," she said. "The play is powerful and original and full of possibilities. Go to him. It must meet with the success you deserve."

Long after he had left her, Jean sat thinking of the play. It had awakened in her such a keen desire for her old work that she could not force it aside. After all, the stage with its varieties and monotonies was a fascination — an irresistible fascination. She began to wonder how she had ever had the courage to leave it at all. It was so much a part of her. She had grown up in it; the very atmosphere was a tonic, a stage setting, an inspiration. But she had promised, and she was very loyal. Her word pledged to Herbert meant a great deal.

Then she began to think of two things at once; that it was time to dress, and that the letter must be answered. That terrible letter! Was it a deliberate attempt on the part of Madam Worthington to make this separation final and complete? Or had Herbert himself prompted the writing of it? Did he wish it because his love for her was dead?

Her face hardened. She dragged herself into her room, tired and dispirited. She must dress for the sitting, for that meant money.

Two days later Richmond called. Jean was out, but Lucie, with a wonderful lightening of her heart, arranged for him to come again the next day.

He was very prompt. It was a habit he required of his people; so he practiced it himself. He seemed overjoyed to see Jean, but he wasted little time on politeness.

"I saw the young man with the Persian name."

"It's a good play," announced Jean.

"Yes and no — depends upon who plays it."

"Well?" queried Jean.

The manager looked at her; looked long and seriously. "You have got the hair for it," he said.

Jean smiled quietly. She knew what was coming. And it sent a glow over her. After all it was agreeable to be wanted. We all like to find a niche that we alone can fill to perfect fullness.

"I've a proposition," went on the manager. "I know you; so does the public. You will carry this thing. With anyone else it would be risky, for you know it's a queer show. You head the company I put out, and we will send it on the road till spring. If it wins, it will open my theatre next fall for as long a run as it will stand."

"And my salary?" put in Jean.

"To start with, one fifty."

"And Omar?"

"Royalties. They all insist on royalties now."

"If I refuse?" she began.

"Can't take the play. Too damned queer. Risky." Richmond shook his head.

"May I have a little time to consider?" asked Jean.

"Not longer than a week. If this thing is a go it's got to start soon."

"I will let you know within a week," she answered gravely.

Lucie lying in her room just beyond, heard the answer. Presently she began to hum, finally to sing. But Jean paid no heed to her sister's voice, although this was the first expression of happiness that had come from her. She went slowly to her desk and reread the letter.

VIII

Jean was dusting. It had been two days since Richmond's interview, and she was still undecided. It made her restless. There was so much to be thought of and considered both ways. She was following out Madam Worthington's theories now. It had been a hobby with the old gentlewoman that house work was the panacea for all ailments.

So she had tucked her hair under a big white cap, smothered her dress in a gingham apron, and was rather amused at the idea that her mother-in-law's foibles should help her at such a time. Jean was hard at it when Carrington came down the stairs. It was easy to distinguish his coming and going from the others. A sudden anxiety to talk over Richmond's offer with him made her open the door. He stood there on the threshold. Lucie lay in his arms. Her eyes were closed and her face perfectly colorless. . . .

"Dick, what has happened?" she cried sharply, an emotion of terror driving out every other thought.

Dick brought the girl in and laid her down before answering. "Fainted," he answered, rather sternly. "Probably she should n't have stood this morning. Iky thinks it 's a reaction from seeing him abruptly and without warning."

Jean was kneeling beside Lucie, bathing her head and chafing her hands. Gradually the languid eyes opened. They looked into Jean's face. "I am better," she whispered, faintly, and smiled as Jean leaned over and kissed her. There was a deal of silent pity in the older sister's face. It was a time Lucie had watched and waited for — the opportunity for a final plea.

"I 've tried to help and wanted to. Really, Cherie, I wanted to. But I am not strong; you see I am not strong." She began drawing her words out.

Jean took the hand Lucie held out and clasped it in both her own. The advantage was still with Lucie.

"I never could stand long at a time. But I did not like to say so before. I did n't want to worry you. You are so good. What can we do if I am not able to earn any more money?"

She had whispered this, but the whisper came distinctly to Carrington. He looked at her and it was a strange gaze, then his eyes went to Jean again. Instinctively the expression softened at once.

She had taken Lucie's head on her lap and was talking to her as she would have talked to a child. "I did not know, dear. I have been blind — selfishly blind. But you must not worry, and you need not stand again."

"Then how will we get on?" The voice was beseeching, but the eyes looked satisfied.

"I will find a way," said Jean.

Then the advantage was gone; but Lucie had accomplished her desire; perhaps succeeded better than she had hoped. She closed her eyes again, and asked for a drink.

It was Carrington who brought it. It was also Carrington who carried her into her bedroom. He asked if he could be of further help, and when he found that he could not, he banged out of the apartment and banged into his studio, muttering unintelligibly.

Iky and Jo in the midst of a tender episode — the climax of the love interest in the book—jumped guiltily at the noise in the next room. They were so upset that they lost the thread of what they were doing.

"What d'you 'spose is up?" said Jo.

"Daubed, probably. Jo, what was this girl saying?" And Jo could n't remember.

While Lucie was sleeping comfortably and quietly, her head pillowed on her hand, and a down quilt warm about her, Omar came. He looked pitiful, and as though he had not slept.

"Have you decided?" he cried. "I had not meant to trouble you. I don't want to influence you. But I could n't wait. I am impatient, cowardly."

Jean was watching him intently. Her face had become pale and strange. She wondered how long it had been since he had had enough to eat. Three good meals a day! The very thought made her hungry. She had not had three good meals a day either for some time past. This prompted her next question.

"It means food, does n't it?" she asked, quietly.

"Yes, but it is n't that. Believe me, it is n't that at all. I am willing to go hungry. I don't want you to consider that; it was only because I was anxious to know — to know if you had decided."

"I have decided." She said quickly, not daring to hesitate. "I am going to accept Richmond's offer."

Omar gave an inarticulate cry. A sound that brought the tears to Jean's eyes. She had not cried for so long that the feeling was strange, and the tears dropped unheeded down her cheeks.

Omar saw them, and he knelt beside her. It was impulse, but thoroughly natural. Still it was such an unusual attitude that Jean smiled in spite of her sympathy with his feeling — and she had entire sympathy.

He did not speak — only kissed her hand. Emotion had blinded him, and somehow his strength was gone. He arose slowly. Then he kissed her hand again and went out softly as though afraid a sound would check the fierceness of his joy. Besides, there was a kind of holiness about the abode of these two women. But he burst into the studio; nothing was sacred here. Carrington stood with his hands in his pockets, puffing at his pipe. Omar caught hold of him, gripping him with the tremendous power that had suddenly possessed him.

"She's decided! She's decided! It will go." He shouted. Iky and Jo, hearing the noise, came in, arm in arm.

Then the four lined up and shouted out the serenade. They sang it twice. It shook the chandeliers and rattled the windows and echoed out through the hall until it came into the apartment below in a torrent of noisy tunelessness.

Jean looked up, and a gleam of happiness lighted her face for a moment. Then she bent over her desk again, unhearing. When she finished, there were two letters. One for Richmond, the other for Madam Worthington.

IX

Richmond put Omar's play into rehearsal before any of the company had expected it. The comedy he had been playing had run itself out, so he decided to send Jean on the road for a month only. After that she was to open in his theater.

Omar was elated over the change. He worked with Jean and he worked with Richmond. It is a great thing to have success within reach; especially when one is tired and cold and hungry.

Late one afternoon when the sun was almost to its setting, and Carrington had stopped painting because the studio was too dark to see color, he heard Omar come in. He walked straight to Dick's room.

"Well, Omar, had a long day of it, haven't you?" Dick called out, glad of company.

Omar came in. One shaft of light fell slantwise across the room. Inadvertently he stopped just where it fell. Carrington was leaning against a chair, and he gazed at his companion's face curiously.

"You are a sight, Omar. What the devil ails you?" His voice was kinder than his words.

"I don't know. I am either insane, or I have found out something damnable. Perhaps it is a mixture of both. Have you any whisky here?"

Carrington went to a cupboard and found a bottle. It was so dark that he spilled a good deal when he poured the stuff into the glass. He swore a little, not at all because he was angry, but because it is the habit of a man to swear when his hand shakes.

Omar drank it without a word. He was silent so long that inaction palled on Dick, and he rolled a cigarette, lighted it and puffed it half away. Carrington never urged a person to talk. There was only a glow in the room when Omar finally spoke. The shaft of light had gone.

"I have either written a play that is hellish, or seeing it put into action has balled me up." He stopped again.

"Get somewhere, Omar," put in Carrington.

"You better take some whisky, too. It will brace you up for what I've got to tell. I know that what I am going to say is hellish, whether it's true or not, and whisky does help."

"I don't want whisky. Speak out or shut up." There was a hint of savageness about Dick. He had grown uneasy. Omar was not usually this way.

"Of course I am going to speak out. That's what I came in here for. I had to speak out. I couldn't keep it bottled up in me. It's the kind of knowledge that makes ghosts. I am going to speak out of course." Then he stopped again.

"For God's sake!" broke out Carrington.

"Don't get savage. It's about Jean."

"What is about Jean?" Carrington tried not to speak overloud. His hands twitched and a strange, creepy feeling went up and down his back.

"I don't know. It's what I think and what I saw, too — for I did see it. You know we have been working hard; she especially. She seems to feel very intensely about the play, and sometimes I think it's more on my account than on her own; the success of it, I mean. She has n't been satisfied with studying just her part; not at all. She has hunted up literature about it. You know the play. I took those people because they never had been handled much before, and it's hard to find original themes — devilish hard. I wish to God though, I had chosen some other. Give me another drink. I have n't had anything to eat all day."

"Then certainly you don't want another drink. Get through, then we will go to dinner."

Omar did not expostulate, but went on, taking up his story where he had left off.

"I never saw a person get so into the spirit of a thing as she has into that part. She says it's because she has studied those people. She says, too, that she feels it all. Their wanderings and loneliness, their suffering, isolation, despair, hopelessness, and all the rest. And I think she does. She told me that when I first read the play to her she could put herself into the character — that that woman lived in her. It was this that made her so sure of its merit. Well, to-day we had a dress rehearsal; make up, costumes, and all the rest of it. You know we leave tomorrow."

Omar gave this as a piece of news. He seemed to have forgotten how they had all watched and waited for the coming of that date.

"It was great! Better than I expected, or hoped, or dreamed! I could n't believe for a long time that it was mine. It was so strange — so grandly strange to think that the words they spoke were my words, the situations my situations.

"Jean was wonderful. She never has acted as she did to-day. She carried the whole company along by her intensity and power and magnetism. Then — then came that last act. That's the one, you know, where she becomes a —— well, one of those people."

He moved his body restlessly and swallowed noisily. His throat was parched.

"Go on," growled Carrington. It was perfectly dark. So dark that there were no shadows, only blackness, and Omar's voice coming huskily from out of its midst.

"When she came on to the stage, there was a strong light. Arranged, of course, to heighten the effect. The glare fell on her from somewhere above. The lower part of the stage was blue — a queer blue that one felt.

"I looked at her once and then I

turned away. I thought something was going to happen, but nothing did. She was going on with her part. There was no hesitation, nothing wrong. So I took courage and looked up. Oh God! Oh God! I hope I will never see again what I saw then. All in a sudden I hated my play. I hated myself. I hated the very sight and sound of a theatre."

The other man made a slight movement. It passed unnoticed. Omar's breathing annoyed Carrington. It seemed always to be coming in, in sharp hisses, as though he were continually catching it. It never went out.

"I don't know how it ended. I stood there like a frozen thing. Yet really I was not cold. I was burning—on fire. My hands were so hot that they pained."

He lifted them now. Raised them slowly, then dropped them again immediately. It was too dark to see.

"The words she spoke had grown to

have no meaning whatever. I heard only vague noises. Noises that came from the roaring of those flames that were consuming me." He huddled himself together rocking his body. "I could n't see, either."

Omar said this with such apparent terror that Carrington gave a step forward. His thought had been to help. But what could he do to help here? He stopped again at once.

"Everything was whirling before my eyes. Going round and round in a sickly, ghastly glare. After it was all over my senses came back a little. I went to Jean. They were all around her, congratulating her. It seemed like congratulating a skeleton on the way it dangled up and down on a wire. I could n't think of anything else, yet that is n't really a comparison. Richmond was crazy. He saw success — money — that 's the only kind of success he understands. I finally got Jean aside. I did n't look at her closely, or even directly.

"'There is danger to you in this,' I said.

"'I know it,' she replied, very calmly. I was n't expecting her to be calm, either.

"'Stop, please stop! I want to starve.' I suppose I said it strangely, for she looked at me with pity and gentleness in her eyes. I know that. I felt it—think of it—pity, gentleness!" He threw out his arms in an abandonment of grief.

"'If there is danger in this, the danger is done,' she said, still calmly. Then I came away. You see I had reached the limit of my endurance. I don't think I said anything more. But I am not sure. I am not sure of anything. Dick, Dick, my heart is broken. Oh, God! Oh, God!"

For a long time there was silence. Carrington's hands were nerveless and there was a blur in his eyes. Presently there came to him a great desire to be alone. The desire grew until it became an actual need. He begged Omar to go to his dinner, but Omar either did not hear or he was too engrossed in his own dreadful thoughts to understand. He did not answer at all. He did not even speak when Carrington left the studio. He said afterward that he did not hear him leave.

Carrington had intended to go for a walk. It seemed to him that a blast of cold air might drive away the feeling in his head. But when he got down stairs he found that he had forgotten his hat. So he climbed up again. He stopped at Jean's apartment. There were no lights there and everything was very quiet. He pushed open the door and went in. He could not see, and there was nothing to hear. He struck a match. Light had become a necessity. Darkness now would always be associated in his mind with that monstrous thing he had just heard. By the flare of the taper he saw Lucie. She was crouched down outside Jean's door. The girl had been crying, and the traces of tears were still visible on her face, but her eyes were closed. From sheer loneliness she had fallen asleep. He shook her and she started up with a cry.

"What is the matter?" he asked sharply.

"I don't know. It is Jean's fault. I have done nothing. Jean has been so odd. I don't know whether she is sick or cross, but I think it's both," she whimpered. "She would n't let me help her, all because I said she looked pale. She was very angry; I don't know why."

"Go in there and see if she is resting," he commanded.

"I can't. She won't let me. I am afraid," expostulated the girl. "She says that I am not to touch her or look at her."

So Carrington knocked — gently — much as a woman might knock. There was no reply. He opened the door softly and listened. Jean's breath was coming and going quickly, but still the regularity of it showed that she slept. Then he closed the door again.

"Go to bed," he said to Lucie, "I'll watch."

Carrington sat there all through the night, wide-eyed, sleepless, until the sky in the east was light with dawn. Then he got up stiffly, and went away; but he never told, and Lucie never told, and Jean never knew.

X

When Jean went "on the road," Carrington did not see her to say good-bye. That may have been the reason why the next month dragged so. She wrote to him once, in answer to one of his letters. They were having immense success, and she was quite well, but would be very glad to get home again. Traveling had lost the spice and newness that it once held for her.

It was a short letter, and on the whole unlike Jean. She was not newsy, not even bright, and there was a strain of cheerfulness that showed distinctly that it was an effort.

All at once everything went wrong with Carrington. He began by having trouble with his models. This hindered him in his work and made him cross. Then the "Plants" decided to take a flying trip west. He insisted that he did not mind being left alone; in fact hinted that it would be a relief. So they took him at his word. They wanted to get local color for a new story. Their last one had been sold, and they were getting fifteen cents on each book. Not enough to make them rich; still it was something and it meant a future.

Dick missed them. Perhaps he had never been in such need of companionship as now. However, nothing would have made him acknowledge this, and nobody guessed it.

He had written to Omar beseeching him to tell the truth about Jean. His letter was four pages of questions and Omar's reply was, as hers had been, a brief account of their successes.

Dick stormed and swore, and wrote again. To this there was no reply. But the four weeks ended and the company came back.

From a feeling of delicacy, Carrington stayed away from Jean's apartment until they should be settled a little. He heard Lucie and Jean go into their rooms, and he had a great longing to hurry after them.

He waited an hour; then the burden of time became too heavy and he took up his hat and his cane. He had an idea that the cane gave him the appearance of having merely dropped in. It was against his principles ever to appear anxious. While he was going down stairs he wondered what had become of Omar.

The door was locked. This was unusual. Always before when they were at home the door was unlatched—and Carrington knew they were at home. He rang the bell, and stood contemplating the head of his cane. He rang a second time. Immediately a maid appeared and said that Madam Halamar was resting and could not be disturbed. She was fatigued from her long journey, and as she was to act that night she wished to feel fresh for her work. It was quite necessary that she deny herself to all callers.

Carrington appreciated all the maid said and really saw the reasons clearly, but he went away with a curious, angry feeling. Omar did not come home at all. He sent a note up to Dick, enclosing tickets for a box, and asking him to be sure and come and bring Iky and Jo; Maurice, too, if possible. He asked, in fact, that Dick make a great effort to bring Maurice. He apologized for not getting up with the tickets himself, but said Richmond wanted him. He did not explain what for.

So Dick sent for Maurice, and they dined together and got to the theatre early. Carrington did not try again to see Jean. Nor did he try to resist the acute terror that had been hovering over him all day. This had settled down heavily upon him, finally enveloping him like a pall, and he could n't shake it off; neither could he force any gaiety through it. It increased until it became actual pain — a pain that was like nothing he had ever experienced before. Coupled with this was a feeling that something unendurable was about to happen.

The theatre filled up rapidly. It was an immense audience. Carrington had expected this, and talked volubly to the doctor about it. He wanted to talk for the relief it brought him. But the words came tumbling from his lips in disconnected sentences, and conveyed nothing very intelligible to Maurice, who was making an attempt to listen. Omar did not appear, but Dick had ceased to wonder at that.

Jean's entrance called forth a storm of applause. For many minutes the audience held the play at a standstill while she acknowledged her welcome. A great lump forced its way up into Dick's throat. Jean was beautiful, more beautiful than he had ever seen her before, but there was a delicate look about her that was new. He noticed Maurice was gazing at her fixedly.

As the play went on both men were

aroused to an intensity of feeling that was not usual with either one. It was a loathsome theme, but wonderfully handled, and Jean's acting was tremendous. Still the dismal foreboding clung about Carrington. He never for one moment lost it.

As the curtain was going up on the last act, Omar stole into the box. Carrington scarcely noticed him. The "blue light that one felt" and the "glare from somewhere above" had caught his attention and was warning him of what was to come. He had suddenly remembered Omar's description of it.

When Jean came on he gasped — a fearful, sickening sound. There was a murmur from many voices all about him, but he did not hear that. He only saw, and saw, and saw, and was so stunned with the awfulness of what he saw, that he knew nothing else. Maurice's eyes were riveted, and his face was drawn into many lines. A tremor had shot up his spine and settled itself somewhere in the base of his brain. Omar sat with his back to the stage, his head sunk in his hands. He looked shrunken and pitiful.

She finished somehow. All through the climax Carrington looked, but saw only THAT. His eyes were burning until the sockets felt like coals, then all at once he closed his eyes, and when he opened them again Jean was gone, the lights were gone, and the people were calling and cheering. But Madam Halamar for whom they called did not come.

Carrington got up and went out of the box, Maurice following him closely. He went back of the stage, going as swiftly and directly as though he had been used to the theatre all his life. Yet he had never been behind the scenes before.

There was a great deal of noise, many people, and some confusion, but he did not stop. He had a glimpse of a dress. Only one glimpse, and in the distance, too, but he recognized it.

Jean was standing in the middle of her dressing room, alone. The light fell on her, not so intensely as that other one "from above," but it was enough. Her face was white — not gray-white, like ashes, but milky, and glaring, and terrible to look upon.

She gave a frightened glance into Dick's face, then held up one arm as if to protect herself.

"Keep away, keep away, don't come near me!" she cried, and her voice was awful to hear. "Don't you see, can't you understand? Look at my face! There is no paint on it. There was no paint on it at all in the last act. I do not have to use paint. It is as I am. It is my mark, do you hear? my mark!"

With a great sob Carrington started toward her.

Then she screamed at him, "No, no, keep back! I am one of them, one of those fearful beings! Look!"

With a move of savage swiftness, the same savage swiftness with which wild creatures shield their young, she tore up the sleeve that fell over her right arm. Maurice leaped forward. All the while her eyes were staring into Dick's. And Omar had crept in, his breath coming in gasps that could be heard above the din of the theatre. His face was scarcely less terrible than hers. There was something inhuman about them both.

Then she moved her arm. The motion was slow and strained. When it was finally raised out of the shadow, they who looked saw that it was withered.

"Oh, God!" moaned Omar, and he reeled back.

"Now you understand, all of you. Go away, go away," she whispered.

"All my life I must cry, 'Unclean! unclean!' Dick, you see, I am a LEPER."

Unconsciously she had held out her arms to him, and with a cry of great love and great tenderness, he sprang to her.

XI

Carrington never understood how he passed that night. In fact, he would never speak of it at all, but sometimes when he thought of it to himself, he wished he was quite clear just what did happen.

About noon the next day Herbert Worthington appeared. His coming was sudden and unannounced. Dick stared at him. He was thin and wretched and unnatural. Dick wondered why he had come, and asked the question; to which Worthington replied, that he had come in answer to a telegram. And he pulled a paper out of his pocket and watched Carrington curiously while he read it.

It was a message sent and signed by Dick. "I suppose I did it," he said, looking up. Then he reread it. "Probably when I sent it I thought it was the proper thing—the only thing. I am not quite certain what I thought, or did, last night."

Worthington evidently expected an explanation, so Carrington attempted one. "I was n't crazy, or drunk, either. I was desperate." He got that far; then he left explanations, and asked a question.

"What is this business that keeps you and Jean apart?" he asked sharply.

Worthington winced. A dull color came into his face, and spread until it covered his face and neck.

"What is that to you?" he demanded.

"Everything, because it is killing her. You did n't know, did you? She is hopelessly ill. Can you understand that? Hopelessly ill. At least it will be hopeless unless a certain series of things can be brought to pass, and the things depend on you. Maurice says he can cure her. He says he is absolutely certain of a complete recovery, providing he can carry out a particular course of treatment."

"Carrington, you must know, you ought to understand, that I am willing. Good God, man, I love Jean! You don't know what I have suffered." Worthington put his hands before his face, and he was not ashamed to have Dick Carrington see the grief which was beyond his control.

"She has grieved for you every minute. She has n't said a word, and I have n't asked any questions; but neither was necessary. I saw and I knew, but I could n't help. No one could ease that sorrow but yourself, and you were silent."

It was such a temptation to Carrington to say harsh things to this man that he abruptly stopped speaking and began to walk around the room. It was not his purpose to quarrel, but he had always considered Worthington a cad, and he wanted to say so to his face.

Worthington sat very still. He had

not raised his head, and he made no effort to speak. Presently Carrington went on.

"Jean is a brick. You don't know just what kind of a woman she is, even though she is your wife. She is generous to a fault, and her sympathy has been her undoing. She is sensitive, too, and proud. I don't mean a false pride, but the other — the kind that makes her respected and loyal and upright and true.

"You don't know, and you probably never will know, what your sending her away has meant to her. How far are you going to carry it?" He stopped in his walk and stood so close to Worthington that when the latter raised his head he found himself looking directly into the other man's eyes.

"I want her now. I have wanted her ever since that day I was so idiotic. I was jealous, Carrington, I know now that it was jealousy. At the time I thought I was being kind — sacrificing myself for her. Instead I was acting like a child. You think badly of me, I can see that, and I don't blame you, but nothing you can think or say will be a circumstance to what I think of myself. I never knew until last night that Jean's request for a divorce was prompted by a letter my mother had written. If I had guessed it, I should have come here long ago. I wanted to come, but I thought she preferred you. I am to blame for everything, except that. I want to tell her so. Where is she?"

Carrington ignored the question. He was determined to finish all that he had to say before he took him to her. "It is Omar's play that has used her up. Maurice calls it a law of suggestion. He is always talking of that law of suggestion. It came from overwork, overstudy, and oversensitiveness. She must have an entire change of climate and an absolute rest, also peace of mind. You can supply these things; Maurice says he can do the rest. He is not mistaken, he is sincere.

It is to be a sort of counter-suggesting, somehow, I don't exactly understand, but he does, and he can do it. I know that. He may be a crank along certain lines, but he always does what he says he can. She must have great kindness and no worries. Your mother, for instance — I don't mean any offence — but leave her at home. Lucie, too; keep her somewhere else. Just you three go: Jean, Maurice, and yourself. It is the only hope — always keep that in your mind — the only hope." Carrington's voice broke. Worthington stood up.

"Take me to her," he said, and Carrington led the way.

Hours afterward Omar found Dick in the studio. Something in the man's face made speech impossible. It was lined and haggard, and somehow he had grown thin.

Omar sat down beside him and put one of his hands on Carrington's shoulder. The act was sympathetic, but unobtrusively so, and Dick turned, gratefully.

"Blues, old man," said he huskily, his voice pathetic for all the attempted cheeriness. "I thought I had passed the age of sentimentality. I should have a broader outlook, for I am old enough."

Omar made no response.

"I know she will get well. She must get well."

Omar gave a slight shudder. He wondered if he would ever be able to think of Jean without that shudder. Then he looked at Dick, and a light of sudden understanding came into his eyes.

"They have gone and she is happy. Half the battle is already won," Dick went on. It seemed a relief to him to speak of her. "Maurice is certain that she will get well. When she saw Worthington, she did not speak. She was pacing her room like a tiger in the stealthiness of her walk. She stopped quickly when he came, as though she were seeing something unreal. Then she went to him without any hesitation. She seemed to forget her horror of coming in contact with another. I suppose the surprise of seeing him made her forget.

"He put his arms around her, and she looked up into his eyes. The expression of her face was what you would expect to find in the face of an angel. The wildness was all gone and the confusion and the desperation. She said 'Herbert,' very quietly, then without the least warning, she fell over in a dead faint, and lay so still and white that I thought she was gone; and Worthington cried.

"He sobbed like a child — great, heavy sobs that shook his whole body. I never saw a man so unnerved. Perhaps he is better than I thought. I believed him a cad. It is rather awful to see a man cry, Omar."

He was not conscious that there were tears in his own eyes.

"And she kissed me good-bye, Omar," he added softly. He said nothing more, and when Iky and Jo came in they found Carrington and Omar sitting side by side. Omar's arm was still around Carrington's shoulder.